Secret Agent Heroes

Felice Arena and Phil Kettle

illustrated by
Mitch Vane

First published in Great Britain by
RISING STARS UK LTD 2004
76 Farnaby Road, Bromley, BR1 4BH

Reprinted 2004, 2005, 2006

For information visit our website at:
www.risingstars-uk.com

British Library Cataloguing in Publication Data

A CIP record for this book is available from the British Library.

ISBN: 1-904591-77-9

First published in 2003 by
MACMILLAN EDUCATION AUSTRALIA PTY LTD
627 Chapel Street, South Yarra, Australia 3141

Associated companies and representatives throughout the world.

Project Management by Limelight Press Pty Ltd
Cover and text design by Lore Foye
Illustrations by Mitch Vane

Printed and bound in Great Britain by
Mackays of Chatham plc, Chatham, Kent

Contents

Nick   Matt

CHAPTER 1

Secret Agents

Best friends Matt and Nick are busy trying out Matt's birthday present—walkie-talkies. Positioned at separate ends of Matt's house, the boys test out the high-tech equipment.

1

Matt "Come in, Nick. Can you hear me? Over and out."

Nick "Loud and clear big buddy. This is secret agent Red Bear. That's affirmative."

Matt "Cool. I mean, copy that, Red Bear. Secret agent Blue Fox here. Anything suspicious happening your end?"

Nick "No. Just your dog, I mean ... a sneaky-looking canine figure eating grass. Nothing else to report. Over."

Matt "Copy that. Meet you at
Headquarters ... no, hold on. Have
spotted something. I've caught
sight of an older female and her
boyfriend."

Nick "You mean your sister."

Matt "Yes, older teenage female."

Nick "What are they doing? Over."

Matt "They're snogging—gross! OTF doesn't realise that she's kissing the enemy—number one enemy agent, Zit Face."

Nick "So, what are we going to do Blue Fox?"

Matt "I have a plan, a mission to break them up. Meet me at Headquarters."

Nick "Affirmative. Um ... Blue Fox?"

Matt "Yes, Red Bear?"

Nick "Where's Headquarters?"

Matt "Inside, in the kitchen."

Nick "Okay. See you there in 0-17 seconds. Over."

CHAPTER 2

Secret Plan

Moments later Matt and Nick meet at Headquarters. They decide to have something to drink and eat before discussing their mission.

Nick "So what's the plan Matt ... I mean Blue Fox."

Matt "It'll be extremely dangerous, the toughest mission we'll ever have to face, Red Bear."

Nick "Cool. I mean, totally copy that, sir."

Matt "You don't have to say 'totally copy that' when you're standing right next to me."

Nick "Copy that. I mean, okay?"

Matt "Right, listen up. The mission is to separate number one enemy agent, Zit Face, from the gross lip lock he has on my sister."

Nick "How?"

Matt "Well, I'm thinking we'll go in there and give him no time to think. Ambush him with water bombs. Follow me."

Matt rushes upstairs to his
bedroom with Nick only a few steps
behind. He rummages through his
cupboard and drawers until he
discovers a couple of unused
balloons.

Matt "We'll fill these up with water."

Nick "That's so cool."

Matt "Don't get too excited. He's one tough agent, that Zit Face. If he spots us before we throw them, we're dead! Are you sure you're up for this, agent Red Bear?"

Nick "Bring it on!"

11

Matt and Nick rush back down to the kitchen to fill the balloons with water.

Matt "You stay here and I'll sneak around to the other side of the house and stop at the back corner just before the garden. So you just wait for my command … on the walkie-talkies."

Nick "Copy that, Blue Fox. I mean, okay."

CHAPTER 3

Mission Beat

Matt and Nick split up with their water-filled balloons in hand. Nick stays put and Matt tiptoes around the other side of the house towards Zit Face and Matt's sister, as planned.

Matt (whispering) "Red Bear, I've made it to the back corner of the house. I'll take a peek and check the status of enemy agent Zit Face. Over. Red Bear? Red Bear? Come in agent Red Bear? You're allowed to say 'copy that'. Red Bear?"

Matt shoves his walkie-talkie back in his pocket, annoyed that Nick hasn't responded and decides to go on with the mission without him. Matt slowly leans forward to catch a glimpse of his sister and Zit Face, only to discover they are nowhere to be seen. Matt is suddenly suspicious—he reaches for his walkie-talkie again.

Matt "Red Bear, come in Red Bear.
I think you could be in danger. Say
something if you can. Red Bear?"

Nick "Blue Fox! Abort mission!
Abort! Abort! Get out of there!"

Matt "What? You're breaking up
Red Bear. What did you say? Over."

Nick "Get out of there! Zit Face saw
me. He caught me before I could ..."

Matt looks up in horror to see that his sister and Zit Face are only centimetres away—and they have Nick's water-filled balloon. They toss the balloon directly into Matt's face, causing him to fumble and drop his own balloon. Zit Face and Matt's sister roar with laughter as they head back indoors. Matt shakes his head, totally soaked and embarrassed.

CHAPTER 4

New Mission

Matt and Nick regroup back at Headquarters.

Nick "Before I knew it, they'd jumped me. I tried to warn you."
Matt "Yeah, well it was too late."

Matt dries himself off with a towel.

Nick "So, what's our next mission?"

Matt "I'm not sure you're up to being a secret agent."

Nick "Why? Just because I got caught by Zit Face? That's not fair. You've got to give me another chance."

Matt "Okay, one more, but if you mess up next time, I'll take your agent badge from you."

20

Nick "I don't have a badge."

Matt "You know what I mean."

Nick "Cool. So what's our next mission Blue Fox?"

Matt "I need to get something very important from my neighbour's garden."

21

Nick "Really? Cool. Is it a secret
document ... or a special spy
gadget ... like a watch that gives
the exact directions of where you
are in the world and acts as a mini
X-ray that can see through walls.
Or is it some amazing clue?"

Matt "No, it's my football."

Nick "Oh."

Matt "I kicked it over into their garden last night. You stay here and look after Headquarters. This is just a mini mission. I can do this one on my own."

23

Matt leaves Nick and heads over to his neighbour's house. He knocks on the door but there's no answer. He decides to go on into their garden, only to discover someone breaking through the back window. Matt quickly ducks behind some nearby rubbish bins, and pulls out his walkie-talkie.

Matt (whispering) "Red Bear? Red bear? Come in Red Bear? Nick? This is serious."

CHAPTER 5

Spy Game for Real

Matt "Nick? Where are you?"

Nick "Sorry Blue Fox. I was caught up with my *own* mission."

Matt "What?"

Nick "I call it Mission-Eat-Your-Mum's-Chocolate-Cake! What's up? Over."

26

Matt "There's a burglar breaking into my neighbour's house."

Nick "That's cool. What's this secret agent's name? Agent Mask Man?"

Matt "Nick, I'm not joking. This is for real. A guy's just broken in. Call the police."

Nick "Copy that big buddy! Your mum's a really good cook you know."

Matt "*Nick!* Call the police or get my mum and tell her."

Nick "Roger, Blue Fox."

27

Matt waits quietly behind his
neighbour's rubbish bins. He peeks
over the top of them and sees the
burglar now coming out the back
door with a television set in his
hands.

28

Matt (whispering) "Red Bear? Have
you called the police? Nick? Come
in Red Bear? He's stealing the TV!"

Nick "Where are you Blue Fox?
Over."

Matt "I'm hiding behind some
rubbish bins in the garden.
Have you called the police?"

Matt suddenly hears the sound of heavy steps walking towards him.

Matt "Nick? Quick! Get help! I think the burglar's heard me. He's coming to get me. I think I'd better run for it."

Matt suddenly looks up to see Nick and a policeman standing over him.

Nick "There you are! This is Officer Handley, Matt. His partner caught the burglar and has just locked him in the back of the police van— it was so cool. You're a hero, secret agent Blue Fox!"

Matt "Yeah? I reckon we're *both* secret agent heroes!"

BOYS RULE!
Secret Agent Lingo

Nick

Matt

affirmative A very long word used by secret agents with a very short meaning—yes!

James Bond Known as agent 007, he's the best secret agent in the world.

secret Information that you find out and don't tell anyone about. But sometimes you can tell your best friend!

spy A person who spies on another person and gathers top secrets.

sunglasses What all secret agents wear to disguise themselves.

33

BOYS RULE!

Secret Agent Must-dos

☞ When you're a secret agent, always wear sunglasses. You don't want anybody to recognise you.

☞ Always carry your walkie-talkie with you. You never know when the spy agency will want you to work.

☞ Carry a notepad with you at all times. Making notes is important.

☞ Use your shed as your spy headquarters.

☞ A secret agent's camera is really small. You should have one to take photos of kids you think might be spies.

☞ Girls mostly work for the bad secret spy agencies. Boys are usually from good spy agencies.

☞ When discussing spy secrets, you need to use a secret code. Make sure you close the curtains in your shed when you're doing this.

☞ Never tell girls a secret. They find it really hard to keep secrets.

☞ Make sure you have a really good spy name when you become a spy.

BOYS RULE!

Secret Agent Instant Info

When spies decode, they work out what a coded message means.

Spies often work undercover in disguise so they can't be recognised.

Ian Fleming wrote the first James Bond novel, "Casino Royale", in 1953.

The most valuable item ever stolen was Leonardo da Vinci's painting of "The Mona Lisa" in 1911.

A bug is a tiny hidden listening device.

 The CIA is one of the largest spy agencies in the world. It stands for Central Intelligence Agency.

 One of the most famous (and funny) television shows about secret agents was called "Get Smart". It was made in the 1960s and is still screened today.

BOYS RULE!
Think Tank

1 Who is agent 007?

2 What is decoding?

3 What is a spy?

4 Where do spies live?

5 When do secret agents spy?

6 Are secret agents good at keeping secrets?

7 Where do you think secret agents keep their secrets?

8 Do you think that you would be a good secret agent?

Answers

8 Yes, the best agent in the world!

7 Secret agents keep their secrets in a safe.

6 Yes, if they can't keep secrets they shouldn't be secret agents.

5 Secret agents spy all the time … so watch out!

4 Spies live in a house.

3 A spy is somebody who finds out some person's secret.

2 Decoding is where you work out what a coded message means.

1 James Bond is agent 007.

How did you score?

- If you got all 8 answers correct, then you should join the secret service.

- If you got 6 answers correct, then maybe you should take a few more lessons.

- If you got only 4 answers correct, then make sure your best friend doesn't tell you any secrets—you might not be able to keep them!

39

Felice →   ← Phil

Hi Guys!

We have loads of fun reading and want you to, too. We both believe that being a good reader is really important and so cool.

Try out our suggestions to help you have fun as you read.

At school, why don't you use "Secret Agent Heroes" as a play and you and your friends can be the actors. Set the scene for your play. Find some props and use your imagination to pretend that you are a secret agent. Maybe you could wear sunglasses.

So ... have you decided who is going to be Matt and who is going to be Nick? Now, with your friends, read and act out our story in front of the class.

40

We have a lot of fun when we go to schools and read our stories. After we finish the kids all clap really loudly. When you've finished your play your classmates will do the same. Just remember to look out of the window— there might be a talent scout from a television station watching you!

Reading at home is really important and a lot of fun as well.

Take our books home and get someone in your family to read them with you. Maybe they can take on a part in the story.

Remember, reading is a whole lot of fun.

So, as the frog in the local pond would say, Read-it!

And remember, Boys Rule!

BOYS RULE!
When We Were Kids

Felice

Phil

Phil "What was your greatest weapon when you were a secret agent kid?"

Felice "My ability to speak one hundred different languages."

Phil "That's a bit ambitious—you can't even speak English properly!"

Felice "Ha, ha … very funny. Well, maybe only fifty langauges then."

Phil "To be honest, I don't think you'd have made a very good spy. You can't even keep a secret."

Felice "Yes I can—try me."

Phil "I can't tell you—it's a secret!"

BOYS RULE!

What a Laugh!

Q Which three letters of the alphabet are robbers scared of?

A I C U.

43

BOYS RULE!

 Gone Fishing

 The Tree House

 Golf Legends

 Camping Out

 Bike Daredevils

 Water Rats

 Skateboard Dudes

 Tennis Ace

 Basketball Buddies

 Secret Agent Heroes

 Wet World

 Rock Star

 Pirate Attack

 Olympic Champions

 Race Car Dreamers

 Hit the Beach

 Rotten School Day

 Halloween Gotcha!

 Battle of the Games

 On the Farm

BOYS RULE! books are available from most booksellers. For mail order information please call Rising Stars on 01933 443862 or visit www.risingstars-uk.com

44